KEEPERS OF THE UNKNOWN:

THE AXEMAN

VOLUME 1, BOOK 1

KEEPERS OF THE UNKNOWN:

THE AXEMAN

VOLUME 1, BOOK 1

Paula Fabiano

ISBN 978-1-62806-472-8 (print | paperback)

Library of Congress Control Number 2026904278

Published by Salt Water Media
29 Broad Street, Suite 104
Berlin, MD 21811
www.saltwatermedia.com

Cover art by Derek Lingle

DEDICATION

Look, Dad! I finally did it!

** fist pump **

PROLOGUE

Montgomery, Alabama, July 1, 2001

A single family home in a small suburban neighborhood. In the living room, a brown-haired man and a brown-haired, five-year-old girl sat around the coffee table, coloring.

"Alright, Phoebe, I'm done. What do you think?"

Phoebe turned her dark green eyes upon the man's picture.

"It's pretty."

The man smiled.

"Yeah? You think?"

Phoebe smiled and nodded.

"Now let's see yours. You done?"

Phoebe grabbed her picture and presented it to the man. It was of a dog laying inside a dog house.

"Oh wow. Would you look at that." The man took the picture and examined it more closely. He looked back at Phoebe. "This might just be the best coloring in the world."

The young girl's eyes lit up at the statement.

"Really?" she responded.

"Really really. In fact, this deserves a special spot on the fridge."

A tall, slender, blonde woman walked into the room carrying a one-year-old baby on her hip. The woman gazed at the man and Phoebe for a few moments, a smile on her face.

"Hey you two," she said. "What are you guys up to?"

"Hi Mommy," Phoebe responded. "Daddy and I are coloring."

Phoebe took her picture back from the man and held it up for her mom to see.

"I see, that's very nice, my love. But it's time for bed now, come on."

The woman held her hand out toward Phoebe.

Phoebe pouted.

"Aw, Mommy, just a little while longer. Pleeeese?"

"I'm sorry sweetheart, it's already late."

"Your Mommy's right, Phoebe" said the man. "We can continue coloring tomorrow."

He stood up and extended his hand towards Phoebe. Phoebe took hold of it, and the man gently pulled her up.

"Can we put the picture up on the fridge tomorrow, too?" Phoebe asked, looking up at her father.

The man smiled down at her.

"Course we can."

They arrived at a bedroom door. The woman gently pushed it open and flicked on the lights. One side of the room was painted light blue and had a crib, rocking chair, changing table, and baby monitor. The other half of the room was painted purple and had a child's bed with a Disney princess blanket and some small beige wooden cabinets for storage. The family of four walked into the bedroom. The woman went over to the crib and gently laid the baby down in it. He stood up at once, holding himself upright by the crib bars and smiling. She ran her fingers through his hair and leaned down and kissed his forehead.

"Goodnight, love," she said.

"Okay Phoebe, our turn. Let's say goodnight to John," said the man. He took Phoebe up in his arms and carried her over to the crib so she could her little brother on the forehead.

"Goodnight, Johnny," she said.

"Night, buddy," said the man. He turned to Phoebe. "Alright, little miss, now it's your turn."

The couple made their way over to Phoebe's side of the room. The woman pulled back the sheets, and the man laid Phoebe down in the bed and tucked her in. He pressed a kiss to her head.

"Good night, baby girl," he said.

The woman did the same.

"Goodnight, honey."

"Goodnight, Mommy, goodnight, Daddy."

The couple smiled and turned to head out the door. The man shut off the lights on their way out and left the door slightly cracked open. The woman wrapped both of her arms around the man's waist and buried her head in his chest. The man wrapped his arms around her waist and kissed the top of her head.

"Finally, they're down," said the woman. Her voice came out muffled.

"I know, finally a little time to ourselves. Top Gun's on tonight. Wanna join me?"

The woman looked up at him.

"Oh, honey, I would love to, but I'm honestly exhausted. I'm just gonna head to bed."

"Okay, sweetheart. Sleep tight."

The man pecked his wife's lips and headed to the living room.

A few hours later, the woman turned over in her sleep, reached an arm out to the opposite side of the bed, and felt only cold, empty space. She partially opened her sleep-laced eyes and saw her husband's spot empty. She sat up and rubbed the sleep from her eyes, slipped out of bed, and made her way out to the living room. It was dark. The only light came from the television.

"Joel?" She softly called out.

Getting no response, the woman moved further into the room and noticed her husband asleep on the recliner. She walked over to him and gently rubbed his shoulder.

"Joel, honey."

Joel slowly opened his eyes.

"Hey, baby," he said, groggily.

"Come on, honey, let's go to bed."

"Hmm, in a minute. Come here."

Joel gently pulled his wife into his lap. He laid his head on her chest. The woman lovingly ran her fingers through his hair. Joel let out a contented sigh. The couple basked in this quite time they had together, something that they loved but rarely got much of these days. A toddler's cry cut across the room. The woman sighed and pulled back.

"I guess I better go handle that," she said.

"Are you sure babe? I can get him if you'd like."

"No no, it's okay, my love. I've got it, you just head on over to bed."

The woman got up and walked to the children's room. John was standing up in his crib, tears streaming down his face. Phoebe was sitting up in her bed, her hands covering her ears, and she had an annoyed look on her face.

"Mommy, he won't stop being a crybaby. Please make him stop."

"I know, my love, it's okay, I'll get him."

The woman strolled over to her son.

Out in the living room, Joel slowly got up from the recliner. He stretched, grabbed the cup from the coffee table, and went into the kitchen. He gave the cup a quick rinse and placed it on the drying rack.

"Mommy!" came Phoebe's terrified scream.

Joel bolted from the kitchen and into the children's room. Laying on the floor right in front of John's crib, bleeding from holes in her lower torso, was his wife.

"Alessia!" cried Joel. He ran to her side and cradled her face. "Oh, no, no." He felt for a pulse–it was there, but thready. His eyes scanned the room for another presence–there was none. "Hang on, Less, hang on. It's gonna be okay." Flames suddenly filled the room.

"Daddy!" Phoebe shrieked. John's screams only got louder.

"Phoebe! Johnny! It's okay, I'm coming."

Joel quickly grabbed John from his crib and pulled Phoebe out of bed. He set John down next to her.

"Take your brother and get as far from the house as you possibly can. Now, Phoebe, hurry!"

Phoebe took John into her arms and fled out of the room. Joel turned back to Alessia, but as he reached for her, he felt the stabbing in his chest, over and over. Joel let out a choked gasp, sank to his knees, and collapsed onto the floor.

Phoebe ran as fast as her little legs could carry her out into the front yard of the house. As she ran, there was a small explosion from John's bedroom window, and the entire house went up in flames. Phoebe turned and watched as it burned.

CHAPTER ONE

Forks, Washington, June 6, 2017

On a cool, sunny day, hundreds of high school seniors sat on a football field, clad in red and white caps and gowns. Up on the stage, the principal, a bald, short, pudgy man, called out names.

"John William Parker."

A boy stood up. He was tall and slender, his thick brown hair was short and shaggy with a fringe, and his eyes were a dark blue. Up on the stands, as well as on the field, voices cheered his name. John walked up on the stage and took his diploma from one of the administrators, a middle aged, skinny, brunette woman. He shook hands with her and walked off the stage, back to his seat. John glanced up at the stands for what seemed to him the hundredth time this morning, hoping to catch a glimpse of his uncle and sister. It was ridiculous, he knew. If they hadn't shown up the first couple of times he looked, they wouldn't be showing up now. John turned his attention back to the ceremony as the principal continued to read out names. One by one students went up and collected their diplomas until finally the last person was called.

"Ladies and gentlemen, it is my pleasure to present to you the class of 2017!" said the principal.

All of the students stood up and cheered as they tossed their caps in the air. An African-American boy and a white boy came up to John. They each threw an arm around his shoulders and brought him close.

"We did it, Johnny, can you believe it?" said the African-American boy. He playfully ruffled John's hair and released him.

"Yeah, who would've thought Jackson would graduate?" John teased the white boy.

"Hey. Come on now," replied Jackson.

Families began to pour onto the field, each of them wanting to take pictures with their loved ones and congratulate them. A couple, the man bulky, the woman short and skinny, walked up to John. The woman gently hugged him.

"Congratulations, sweetheart," she said.

"Yeah, congrats, son," said the man.

"Thank you, Uncle Rob, Aunt Laura." *At least some people I care about are here for me.*

Laura also took a turn hugging John's two friends.

"Jackson, Eric. Congratulations, you two."

"Thanks, Mrs. Murphy," said Eric.

"Yeah, thanks, Mrs. M.," said Jackson.

"Well, my folks are waiting for me so I've got to run. But, John, we can count on you at the bonfire tonight, right?" Eric asked.

"Yeah, for sure," John replied.

"I should be finding my parents too. See you tonight, John," said Jackson. "Bye Mr. M., Ms. M."

"Bye, Jackson," said Rob and Laura.

"Oh, John, we should get a few pictures together," said Laura. "We can do one with Rob and I separately, and one with all three of us."

John smiled. "Sure thing, Aunt Laura," he replied. "Whatever you want." He loved that Rob and Laura always made an effort to be there for him and support him, while his blood family could seem to care less.

"Rob, you can go first. Stand next to John."

Laura ushered Rob over to John and directed him where to stand.

"Okay you two, smile in three... two... one...."

John readied himself in his bedroom at Rob and Laura's house. He opened the top drawer of his dresser, which had two photos, one of him and his sister when they were kids, and one of their parents. He grabbed a white t-shirt, slipped it on, and gave himself a once-over in the mirror. Satisfied, he nodded and went downstairs. Laura and Rob were by the front door, and judging by the way they were dressed, John knew it was their weekly date night.

"Alright, John, Aunt Laura and I are heading out," said Rob.

"Cool, I'm heading out too."

"You can take my car," said Rob. He grabbed two keys from off the key rack. "Catch!"

"Thanks!"

The three walked out the door.

"John, lock up for us, will you, dear?" said Laura.

"Will do."

"Thank you, dear," replied Laura. "And have fun tonight."

"Yeah, you guys, too. Don't stay out too late!"

"Ha!" responded Rob, "we should be the one's telling you that."

John locked the door and got into Rob's car. He sent a quick message to Eric and Jackson in the group chat to let them know he was on the way.

John parked. The whole graduating class must've been there, judging by how many cars there were. He got out of the car and made his way down to where the beach was illuminated by the many bonfires. He spotted Jackson and Eric among the crowd, conversing with one another, each with a beer in hand. He strolled down to them.

"There he is!" cried Jackson, once he caught sight of John.

"Hey, guys."

"Finally, man," said Eric. "How are Jack and I here before you? You're usually the punctual one."

John shrugged. "Lost track of time. How long have you guys been here?"

"Not long, we got here just a half hour ago," Eric answered.

"Well come on, let's get you a beer," spoke Jackson. He wrapped an arm around John's shoulder and, together with Eric, escorted him over to a cooler.

"You know if the cops show up here we're busted right?" John said.

"Ah, come on, man, what are the chances of them actually doing that?" said Eric. "Plus, it's graduation night, it's a party. Live a little."

"You heard the man," said Jackson. "What's your poison? We've got Bud Light, Heineken, and Corona."

"Bud Light's fine."

Jackson grabbed a can of Bud Light and carefully threw it to John. The three sauntered over to the fire and plopped down on the sand. John cracked open his can of beer and took a sip. Normally he wasn't one for breaking the law, but he figured what the heck? Tonight's a special night.

"I believe a toast is in order, boys," said Eric, as he raised his can. "To this new chapter in our lives."

"Hear, hear," added John. They all bumped their cans together and took swigs of their beers.

"Oh, and let's not forget, John's awesome college victory."

"Woo! Yeah! Go John," cheered Jackson.

"Ah, it's not that big of a deal," said John. He didn't like when people made a huge fuss over him.

"What?" Eric responded, a you-got-to-be-kidding-me look on his face. "Man, quit being humble. You got a full ride to Harvard University, plus graduated a year early. That's huge."

"How's it feel, being your family's golden child?" asked Jackson.

"Ah, they don't know about the Harvard thing" responded John. "I haven't gotten around to telling them."

"What? Why not? Man, I would be gloating," said Jackson. He took a big gulp of his beer.

"Because my family is kind of complicated. Ever since we were kids, my uncle's expected my sister and I to go into the family business. Phoebe I know for sure is gonna follow in his footsteps, she doesn't see herself doing anything else. Me, on the other hand, I knew I wanted to do something different with my life, and I made that clear to my uncle several times, but I don't think he's ever really listened. Now that it's officially set in stone, that I'm not gonna be joining them, they're not gonna be too thrilled. Well, my uncle for sure won't be. Phoebe will be upset for a little while, but eventually she'll get over it and support me in her own way."

"Oh yeah, you said your family are traveling aircraft mechanics, right?" said Jackson.

"Yep," said John. He was lying. He couldn't exactly tell Jackson and Eric, or anyone for that matter, the truth about what his family did. It would be too dangerous, and, plus, it would sound so loony that they wouldn't believe him anyways.

"You know, in the two years we've known each other, you've rarely brought up your family," stated Jackson, taking another sip of his beer.

John also took a drink from his can and shrugged. "Like I said, complicated."

"Well, regardless, we're proud of you, John," said Eric. "And hey, if your family can't see the fact that you're on to bigger and better things, screw 'em."

"Just don't forget about little old us when you're over at Harvard being a big shot," joked Jackson.

John chuckled. "Never. I'll invite you guys over to my dorm once I'm settled."

"Hells yeah," said Jackson. "Party at Harvard."

The three passed the rest of the time drinking, talking, laughing, and just being carefree. Jackson got up to get some beer, asking John and Eric if they wanted any. John refused, he didn't want to drink too much tonight. He had to drive home afterwards and didn't want to risk anything happening, especially in Uncle Rob's car. John stared out at the ocean, watching the waves crash onto the shore. He felt Eric bump his shoulder and turned to look at him.

"There's your girl," said Eric. He directed John's attention over to a long table that had a punch bowl along with an assortment of foods. By it was a beautiful blonde girl of short stature surrounded by a group of friends.

John rolled his eyes. "She's not my girl."

"Not yet. You should go talk to her."

"What? No way."

"Why not? Man you've been pining over this girl since the beginning of the year. Go talk to her, this might be your last chance."

"Who we talking about?" asked Jackson. He had returned with the beers. He handed one to Eric.

"John's girl, Olivia."

"Not my girl."

"Ohhh. You should go talk to her."

"That's what I said!"

"Alright alright cut it out. That's not gonna happen".

"Hey Olivia!" Jackson cried out.

"Jackson!" John hissed, standing up. "What are you doing?"

"Being your wingman," Jackson replied.

Olivia looked around for whoever called her.

"Over here!" said Jackson.

Olivia caught sight of Jackson. He waved her over. She turned to her friends, mouthed something, and began walking towards John and his friends. John instantly became panicked, though he tried not to show it. Olivia stopped in front of them.

"Yes?" she said.

"My friend John here has something he'd like to say to you," said Jackson.

Olivia turned her gaze upon John..

Great, now I have to think of something fast without sounding like a total idiot. Damn you, Jackson. Olivia raised an eyebrow, waiting. John wracked his brain for a topic of conversation. Let's see...what's something he knew about her? Anything?

"Uh, I just wanted to say congratulations on getting into Seattle University." Realizing he sounded like a total creep, seeing as they had never spoken to each other until now, he quickly offered up an explanation as to how he knew that. "I overheard you telling your friends about it in the school cafeteria."

Olivia smiled. "Thanks. John, right? I'm pretty sure we were in the same history class."

"Yeah, that's right."

"Hey Eric," said Jackson. "Why don't we have a little race? Last one to the water has to do the other's toilet scrub duties at the fire house." He gave Eric a look that said come-on-let's-leave-them-alone.

Eric, getting the drift, stood. "Oh, you're so on," he replied.

The two sprinted down the beach, Eric way ahead of Jackson, who was struggling to catch up. Just as it seemed Eric was going to win, Jackson caught up to him. He shoved him to the ground and darted for the shore, raising his arms in a gesture of victory once he reached it. Eric pulled himself off the sand, charged at Jackson and tackled him into the water. John and Olivia laughed at the whole ordeal.

"Those guys are nuts," Olivia commented.

"Yeah, but they're good people."

"So, John... we've been in the same class together the entire school year, how come we're just now speaking?"

"I tend to get nervous around pretty girls." A sudden shock came over John at the realization he had said that out loud.

Olivia smiled teasingly at him.

"So you think I'm pretty, huh?"

"No... I... Uh.,"

"So you don't think I'm pretty?"

"No! I mean I do but—"

Olivia wrapped her hand around the back of John's neck and brought him in for a kiss. For a second, John froze but then quickly kissed back.

"You're cute when you ramble," Olivia whispered as they pulled away. "Give me your phone."

John reached into the pocket of his shorts and took out his phone. He handed it to Olivia. She typed in her number and returned the phone to John.

"Call me sometime." She went back to rejoin her friends.

John looked down at his phone and beamed.

"Yes!" he softly cried to himself. He dropped the phone on the sand and went to join Jackson and Eric at the shore.

"So, how'd it go?"

"I got her number," John said, grinning. "And we might've kissed."

"My boy," said Eric, slapping John on the shoulder.

"Let's freaking go, man," said Jackson. Both he and Eric then tackled John into the water. *Best night of my life,* thought John as he wrested with Jackson and Eric.

John pulled into Laura and Rob's driveway. Laura's car wasn't there, which meant they were still out. *Must be having fun, John thought. They're usually never out this late.* He let out a sigh, completely exhausted from the night's excursion. He couldn't wait to get out of these wet clothes, have himself a nice warm shower, and just relax for the rest of the night. He hopped out of the car and made his way inside the house, locking the door behind him.

He was about to go upstairs, but something stopped him in his tracks, something alarming. The kitchen light was on, and it sounded like someone was messing around in there— an intruder, but there were no signs of a break in. John quietly opened the door to the hallway closet and grabbed the rifle Rob kept tucked away in there. He tip-toed into the kitchen, rifle raised, taking care not to make any noise so as to not alert the intruder. The fridge door was wide open and someone was hunched over, rummaging through it.

"Don't move," said John. "Who are you? And how'd you get in this house?"

The person looked up over the fridge. It was a young woman. Her dark brown hair was long and wavy and came down to her shoulders, and her eyes were a baby blue color. She grinned at John and straightened up. She was tall, for a woman.

"Woah, easy there, cowboy. It's just me."

"Phoebe?" John exhaled and lowered the rifle, relief flooding his body. "You scared the crap out of me. What are you doing here?"

"Well, I was looking for a— why are you all wet?"

"I was at a thing." John set the rifle against the wall. "You didn't answer my question. What are you doing here? Wait a minute, where's your car? I didn't see it out front."

"Ah, I parked it a ways from the house. Wanted to surprise you."

"Consider me surprised." *And not in a good way. Phoebe showing up here out of the blue must mean she wants something.*

Phoebe and John heard the front door open.

"John?" Laura's voice flooded the hallway.

"Kitchen!" John called back.

Her light footsteps approached.

"How was your— Phoebe!" cried Laura, floored to see the young woman.

"Hey, Aunt Laura," said Phoebe. She walked up to the woman and gave her a hug. "How are you?"

"Good. A bit shocked to see you all the way out here. John, why didn't you mention Phoebe was coming?" asked Laura.

"I'm just as surprised as you are. Where's Uncle Rob?" John responded.

"Oh, a friend of his called last minute asking for help. Car troubles. He should be back soon, though."

"I'm sorry, Aunt Laura, I need to borrow my brother for a sec to speak about a private family matter, and it's pretty urgent. So John, if you will?"

Phoebe started towards the little door in the back of the kitchen near the sink with a window that gave a clear view of the backyard.

"Hold on," said John.

Phoebe halted in her steps and turned around.

"Aunt Laura is just about family as anyone. So whatever family matter you have to tell me, you can say it in front of her too."

"Alright—"

"Actually," interjected Laura, "if you guys prefer to talk in private I can step out."

"No, no, Aunt Laura it's okay," said Phoebe. "It's

your house, I wouldn't dream of asking you to step out. So uh, Uncle Daryl's missing. I haven't heard from him in about a month, and whenever I try calling, I get nothing."

"So he's picking up extra shifts at the hangar. He'll stumble in sooner or later."

"Uncle Daryl went *hunting*. You know, with Jim, Samuel, and Morgan."

Upon hearing that his uncle was hunting, John's blood immediately ran cold. He was silent for a second, just staring at his sister.

"Aunt Laura, could you excuse us? Phoebe and I are just gonna step outside for a moment."

"Of course," replied Laura.

Phoebe and John walked out into Laura and Rob's backyard through their kitchen door.

"I need you to hit the road with me, Johnny. Tonight. I need your help to find Uncle Daryl, we can't waste anymore time," said Phoebe as soon as the door shut behind them.

"What?" John responded incredulously. "Phoebe, come on. You can't just break into Aunt Laura and Uncle Rob's house late at night like this and expect me to just up and leave with you. It's not gonna happen. I've had a long day, I'm soaking wet, I'm tired. I just want to shower and get some sleep."

"I don't think you're hearing me Johnny. Uncle Daryl's missing. Do you even care?"

"Of course I do. But this isn't the first time he's done something like this, remember? He goes missing on cases pretty much all the time, and guess what? He's always fine."

"No, not this time. Something's wrong. I can feel it. Uncle Daryl's in real trouble Johnny, and we have to find him."

"Okay Phoebe, even if you are correct, what good is leaving late at night like this gonna do?"

"What's wrong with you, huh? I'm telling you Uncle Daryl's in trouble and you're coming up with all of these excuses not to go help me find him. After everything he's done for you, for us—"

"Everything he's done *for me?*" John scoffed, he couldn't believe what he was hearing. Did Phoebe not experience the same childhood he had? Did she have a different uncle? "I'm sorry, the only thing Uncle Daryl has ever done for me is set the land speed record for the world's most screwed up childhood."

"Come on John, don't be over-dramatic."

"No, it's true, Phoebe, and you know it. The way we were raised after Mom and Dad were killed, and Uncle Daryl's obsession with finding the witch who killed them. And even after we found and killed the damn woman, it didn't end there. There were still more tests on the occult, more weapons training, more road-trips across the country to hunt down all of those freaky creatures."

"Those road-trips helped a lot of people along the way, too."

"You think this is the kind of life Mom and Dad would've wanted for us? Man, Phoebe, we never got the chance to just be regular kids."

Phoebe rolled her eyes.

"Regardless, he's still our uncle, and he's the only father we got. I need you, I can't do this without you."

"Yes, you can."

"Yeah, well I don't want to."

John looked down and sighed, thinking on whether or not he should do this.

"Alright, fine. What was he hunting?"

"Let's go down to the car. I have all the information there."

They proceeded around the side of the house and down to the street, which was illuminated by street lamps. They walked in silence until they came up to a light blue 1982 Oldsmobile Delta 88 Royale Brougham sedan with a white roof.

"Oh, hold on a sec," said Phoebe. "I got you something."

"You got me something?"

"Yeah, it's your graduation gift."

Phoebe opened the left side rear door of the car and brought out a nice-looking bracelet and a brown Carhartt duffle bag that had "Johnny" embroidered on it. She handed the gifts to John, who examined them.

John smiled at his sister. "Thank you, Phoebe. I appreciate this."

"Ah, it's no problem. Sorry I didn't make it, I was working my own gig, this poltergeist in Pennsylvania, and it ran a little longer than expected."

"Wait a minute," said John as he slipped on the

bracelet. "Uncle Daryl let you go on a hunting trip by yourself?"

"I'm twenty-one, dude."

John and Phoebe heard footsteps headed their direction. They turned and saw Rob coming up to them.

"Uncle Rob, hi," greeted Phoebe.

"Was your friend's car an easy fix?" John asked. "Aunt Laura told us you had to go help a friend out. You're back pretty fast."

"No, no I didn't have time to look at it tonight. We just brought it down to my shop," replied Rob. "Phoebe, I'm glad to see you, though I wish it were under better circumstances. Laura told me that you came here because Daryl is on a hunting trip and is missing? Do you know what he was hunting?"

"We were just getting to that, actually," said John, looking to Phoebe to explain.

"I'm not sure exactly what he was hunting. But about a month ago I was in Vermont helping out with a case when I got a call from Uncle Daryl, and he told me he was gonna go off on a case. Never told me what, though. That was the last time I heard from him for a while, until, a week ago, when he sent me a text of some random location. I tried calling him again and again, but he wouldn't pick up. So I figured he sent me the text for a reason right? So I started doing some digging on the location, and I found this...." Phoebe opened the trunk of the car. It was spacious and contained a collection of weapons, ranging from guns to knives. "Let's see, where the heck did I put that thing? Ah, here we go." She grabbed a manila folder and pulled some papers out of it. "About a month ago, this girl, Anna Hendrix, was found dead in her car on some bridge here in Washington. No sign of the head, cut clean off."

Phoebe handed one of the papers to John. It was a printout of an article from a website called *The Herald*, headlined "Murder at McArthur bridge" and dated April 30, 2017. It included a picture of a silver sedan on what seemed to be a small, local bridge along with a photo of a blonde-haired young woman. John glanced over the printout before passing it to Rob.

"Serial killer, maybe?" John suggested.

"That's what I was thinking at first, but look, here's another one from January. Another in November '16, December '13, July '10, April '08, May '04." Phoebe tossed down a bunch of *The Port Townsend Daily* news articles one by one, some with the dates she'd mentioned and others with dates she hadn't. "There's been at least twelve of them in the past fourteen years. I noticed as I poked around a bit more that this has started to happen more often, so I put two and two together and realized this is what Uncle Daryl went to check out. Something must've gone wrong while he was out there, so I figured that's why he sent that text, it was sort of an SOS."

"Where is this at?" asked Rob.

"Port Townsend, Washington. Just a little over two hours from here."

A sharp pang of hurt rose in John's chest. His

uncle had been so close by, he couldn't have dropped by for a quick visit? To at the very least say hi? He'd been living with Laura and Rob for the entire school year, and not once did his uncle make an effort to call him, to check up on him and see how he was doing. They hadn't had any form of contact whatsoever. But, as he always did whenever it came to any hard feelings about his uncle, John quickly suppressed it. *Come on, don't let it get to you,* John told himself. *You should be used to it by now, you know what he's like. He did this last school year, too.*

"This text lead to any specific area in Port Townsend? Like a park, theater, or something?" asked Rob.

"Matter of fact, it did," responded Phoebe. "Some sleazy little motel."

"Excellent. I suggest we head there first. Maybe we can find some clues as to your uncle's whereabouts," said Rob.

"Hold on. We?" said John.

"Yes, we. I'm coming with. What'd you guys think I'd leave you hanging? Let you deal with a thing like this all by yourselves? Ain't gonna happen."

"Uncle Rob, we appreciate it but we can't ask you to do something like this," said John.

"Good thing I ain't asking. Look, Daryl is my best friend, he's like a brother to me. A very irritating, pig-headed S.O.B of a brother, but he'll always be family. And if there's a chance he is in trouble, then it's my obligation to help him. So I'm going."

"Alright, if you insist. But are you sure you can handle it? You've been out of the game a while," Phoebe said.

Rob scoffed. "I can still run circles around you, girl. Besides, remind me again of who it is you and your uncle call every time you need advice on cases? Now, I suggest we get a move on. The longer we sit around, the worse our chances of finding your uncle become. Just give John and I a moment to get packed, and then we'll be good to go." Rob looked to John. "Oh and you should probably get changed into something dry, son. Can't go anywhere like that."

"Gee thanks, Uncle Rob. Never even crossed my mind to do that," John sarcastically responded.

"Just looking out," said Rob as he started the walk up the street to the house.

CHAPTER TWO

John, now changed into some fresh clothes, walked downstairs, the brown Carhartt duffle bag Phoebe had just given him in hand. He heard Laura and Rob's voices coming from the living room and made his way in there. Phoebe was sprawled out on the couch, while Rob and Laura conversed in the middle of the living room. Rob carried a backpack on his shoulders.

"I still don't feel good about you guys leaving late at night like this, Rob," said Laura.

Rob placed his hands on Laura's shoulder's and rubbed them soothingly.

"Sweetheart, I already told you, we'll be fine. We'll be back in a few days, alright?"

Laura gazed out at the room and sighed worriedly, she looked back at Rob.

"And all of this is about Daryl? Is he okay? You still haven't told me what exactly happened. Phoebe mentioned he was hunting something?"

"Oh yeah he had some time off from work and decided to take a trip to the woods with a couple of his buddies to shoot some deer. Cell reception out there is bad, and he most likely lost track of time. We're just gonna go out there to check on him is all."

John cleared his throat, announcing his presence. "Um, is everyone good to go?"

Phoebe stood. "Yep" she said. "Uncle Rob?"

"Yeah," responded Rob. "Okay, sweetheart, we've gotta go. I'll see you soon."

He kissed her.

"Well, I love you guys. Be safe," said Laura.

"Don't worry, Aunt Laura, we always are," said Phoebe.

Phoebe and John took turns hugging Laura and followed Rob out the door.

"Oh, and be sure to call me!" Laura called out as the door slammed shut.

Port Townsend, Washington, June 6, 2017

A car drove up to an old bridge. Inside were two brunette young women.

"The lighting on this bride is ass," said the passenger.

"Hold on, let me turn on my high beams," said the driver. She flicked the stick next to the steering wheel, and the path ahead of them was more illuminated. "There, much better."

"God, I hate driving on McArthur bridge. Especially late at night like this," said the passenger.

"I know, I do, too. Even more so now with all these murders happening here."

The passenger groaned. "Ugh, girl, don't remind me. Can we not bring that up as we're on the bridge?"

The driver laughed. "How are you and Marcus doing?"

"Same old, same old. I'm thinking of ending it with him though, officially."

The driver briefly glanced at the passenger. "About damn time. He's been nothing but a problem. He's adding nothing positive to your life whatsoever."

"He really isn't. I'm just so tired of the constant back and forth. I'm entirely too grown for this."

"That, and you deserve so much better."

The dim lights on the bridge suddenly began to flicker, startling both women.

"What the heck?" said the passenger. "Uh oh, I don't like this."

"Girl, it's nothing. You know how old this bridge is. These lights aren't even LEDs, they're probably ready to burn out or something," said the driver.

"Still. Hurry up and get off this bridge, please."

The driver rolled her eyes at her friend and floored the gas pedal, but the engine stalled. She started it again; the car lurched forward a few feet, sputtered, and stalled once more.

"What in the hell is happening?" the driver muttered.

"Try it again," said the passenger.

The driver turned the key, but the engine only made a weak turnover sound.

"Oh no. No, no, no! This cannot be happening right now," cried the driver. She slammed her hands down on the steering wheel in frustration.

"Hold up, you see that?" Something at the end of the bridge had caught the passenger's attention.

"Down there" the passenger pointed at the end of the bridge.

"Oh, shit."

At the end of the bridge stood a tall, broad-shouldered person, maybe a man, but it was too dark to be sure. In the person's left hand was a long axe that touched the ground. After a long moment, the person just disappeared, as though no one had ever been there.

"What the fuck?" cried the passenger. "Hell, no. Get us out of here, now!"

The driver cranked the engine, but it made the same struggling noise as before.

"Ugh!" screamed the driver. She turned to face her friend. "Okay, we're gonna have to run for it. On the count of three you open your door, I'll open mine, and we'll head for the end of the bridge."

The passenger nodded in agreement.

"One, two, thr—ahh!"

The person was now right in front of the car. In the light, the two women could see it was a man. Short, brown hair poked out from under a baseball cap, and his beard was stubbly. Everything seemed to go still. The young women sat frozen in fear as the man eyed them. He gave them a menacing smile and began to circle the car, dragging the axe behind him, creating a clunking sound.

"Oh my God, Jennifer," whimpered the passenger.

"It's gonna be okay, Macy." replied the driver, her voice shaky.

The man had made a full circle around the car. In a last ditch effort, Jennifer reached for the key and continued to try and start the car, but to no avail. The man circled the car two more times and then vanished just as before.

"Where'd he go?" asked Macy, glancing around.

"I don't know."

Jennifer glanced in the rear-view mirror. There the man was, in the backseat. She let out a scream. Macy quickly faced her.

"What? What is—ahh!"

She too now noticed the man. In a flash, the man swung his axe at Jennifer and sliced her head clean off. Blood spattered everywhere, most of it hitting Macy's face. Macy let out a horrifying scream at seeing her friend's head fall from her body. The man raised his axe at Macy. He brought it down. Macy was quick to react, and she attempted to reach for the axe in order to try and grab it from him, but it ended up slicing into her arm.

"Argh!" Macy bellowed.

The man swung the axe at her again. Macy swiftly ducked. Using her good arm, she quickly reached for the door handle behind her and flung the car door open. She hurried out of the car and tumbled flat on her back onto the bridge. She looked up at the sky, panting heavily, trying to catch her breath. The man right above her, he raised the axe above his head, and right as he brought it down on her, Macy channeled as much force as she could muster and kicked the axe's handle so hard that it flew clear out of the man's hand and landed on the other end of the bridge. The man growled maliciously at her and went for the axe. Macy clambered to her feet and, clutching her heavily bleeding arm, made a break for it, running as fast as her legs could carry her.

"Help! Help!" She cried.

Macy made it to the end of the bridge. She continued running until exhaustion mixed with blood loss caught up to her and she collapsed face-first onto the dirt road.

Phoebe pulled the Oldsmobile into the parking lot of a small, run-down motel. The flickering letters on the tall sign read Delta Motel.

"Alright, this is it," Phoebe announced as she put the car in park. "Everyone ready? Let's go."

She opened the car door, hopped out, and walked to the back of the car. Arthur and Tom followed suit. Phoebe opened the trunk and grabbed her and John's bags.

"Here you go, Johnny," said Phoebe as she tossed John his bag.

John caught it and rolled his eyes. He detested that nickname, it made him feel like an inferior little kid. "It's John, Phoebe. How many times do I have to tell you not to call me that?"

Phoebe merely ignored him and loudly shut the trunk. "What was that, Johnny? Couldn't hear you. Shut the trunk too loud."

John sighed. "Whatever. Let's just go."

The three marched up to the motel's front office. They entered inside. Behind the counter sat an older, pudgy woman with gray hair and moon-shaped glasses. They approached her and set their things down. She looked up from the newspaper she was reading, eyes peering over her glasses.

"Hi, welcome to Delta Motel. May I help you?" she greeted.

"Yes," said Phoebe. She took out her phone, pulled up a recent picture of Daryl, and presented it to the woman. "Do you recognize this man, by any chance?"

"Yes. He's a guest here."

"Is he still staying here?" asked John.

"I would assume so. He never checked out, his room is still booked for the next two weeks or so."

"Have you seen him around recently?" John asked.

"Honestly, I can't recall. I mostly only see guests during check-in and check-out."

"Are you sure there's nothing you can remember at all?" responded John. "We're sorry for bombarding you with all these questions, it's just that this man is a close family friend, and we haven't heard from him in quite a while. He mentioned to us that he was staying here so we decided to take a quick trip down to check on him. We're really worried about him, so anything you can tell us would be extremely helpful."

The woman exhaled and looked up to the ceiling, as though trying to wrack her brain. "Um...oh, yes! I remember now. I last saw him around a week ago, caught a glimpse of him leaving his room. Seemed to be in a bit of a hurry, too."

Phoebe, John, and Rob shared a look.

"Is there any way you can tell us what room he's staying in?" John asked.

"I'm sorry sir, I can't do that."

Rob placed his arm on the desk and leaned in. "Listen," he said. "We know it must seem sketchy, three people coming up to you and asking all sorts of questions about one of your guests. But we believe our friend may have gotten himself into some sort of trouble, and we really need to see him and make sure he's okay. So it's imperative that you tell us his room number. Please."

"I'm really sorry sir. but—" the phone rang. "Excuse me a moment." The woman answered the phone. "Delta Motel, how can I help you? Can't it wait a few minutes? I'm with some people right now.... Okay, fine. I'll be right there." The woman hung up and stepped out from behind the counter. "I'm sorry, but I have to step out for a bit. There's something with a guest I have to see to."

"No, no. Take your time," responded Phoebe. She eyed the receptionist exiting the building. "Well that was lucky." She quickly walked behind the counter and got onto the computer, trying to get information on her uncle's room number. Fortunately for her, it wasn't password protected.

"How do you know what name Uncle Daryl used?" asked John.

"If I'm guessing correctly, it's the one on his most recent credit card."

"Let me guess, the last poor dead person's social security number you guys were using ran its course, so you had to buy another one from that one sketch-ass guy?"

"Right you are, Johnny."

"I still think it's seriously messed up you guys do that."

"Gotta make money some way."

"You could always try, I don't know, getting a real job."

"Hunting is our job, and the pay is ass. Besides, those people are dead, what good is their social security to them now?"

John shook his head. This was just another one of the many reasons he wanted to leave this lifestyle.

Rob briefly glanced out the window. "She's coming back," he warned Phoebe. "Hurry up, get out of there."

"Okay. I got it. Burt Jacobson, room 308." Phoebe sprinted out from behind the counter and rejoined John and Rob.

"I'm sorry about that," said the woman as she entered the building and walked back behind the counter. "A guest had an issue with their toilet," she sighed, "and of course this happens on the one day my only maintenance man is out. Now, as I was saying, I can't give out guest information. But, if you would like, you can leave a message, and I'll give it to him whenever I see him. In the meantime, is there anything else I can help you with?"

"Actually, yes, since we're here," said Phoebe. She withdrew her wallet from her black duffle bag, pulled out a credit card, and tossed it on the counter. The name on the card was Sarah Drew. "Two rooms, please."

The woman took the card. "How long?" she asked.

"Make it a week," said Phoebe.

The woman nodded and began to input information to the computer. She gave the card back to Phoebe and turned around and grabbed two room keys from off a rack. She passed the keys to them. "Enjoy your stay."

"Will do."

They grabbed their stuff and left the building.

"Hey, how much I owe you for that room?" Rob asked Phoebe.

"Don't worry about it," responded Phoebe.

"You sure?"

"Yeah, come on, let's get to Uncle Daryl's room."

They stood in front of room 308. Phoebe looked around to make sure no one was nearby then proceeded to pick the lock. She pushed the door open, and they stepped inside. Rob flicked on the lights. They walked through the room, examining it for signs of anything unusual, but it was pretty nice and well kept. Nothing seemed out of the ordinary. John stopped in front of a bulletin board which had printouts of the exact same articles Phoebe had shown him earlier.

"Seems as though Uncle Daryl got about as far as you did, Phoebe," John said.

"What are you talking about?" responded Phoebe, her back to him.

"Here," said John. She turned to him, and he pointed behind him to the bulletin board.

"Huh," responded Phoebe.

Rob noticed an envelope on the nightstand. It had Phoebe written across it. He picked it up. "There's an envelope here," he announced. "Phoebe, it's addressed to you." He held it out towards her. She took it, opened it, and pulled out the contents, skimming over it.

"It's a letter," she said. "From Uncle Daryl."

"Uncle Daryl?" John hurried over to her side. "What's it say?"

"'Phoebe, had to go help an old buddy of mine with a case in Alaska. Couldn't finish the job over here, so I'm passing it to you instead. It's why I sent you the text with the location. I'll call you as soon as I finish up over here, and we'll go pick up Johnny from Rob and Laura's house. Daryl.'"

John huffed in irritation. "So he's not in trouble after all. He's just being an asshole, as freaking usual."

"Okay, okay. But look, it's not all bad. At least we know he's fine," said Phoebe, trying to bring some light to the situation.

"Yeah," John scoffed. "And this isn't something he could've told you when he sent that text or, you know, picked up the numerous calls you made to him and explained then? No, instead he had us believe something had happened to him and led us all the way out here for nothing."

Phoebe sighed. "John, I get it, okay, I do. But us being here isn't totally for nothing—"

"No Phoebe, I'm tired of you making excuses for him. I'm done. Sorry for getting you mixed up in all of this, Uncle Rob. We'll get you home in the morning."

"First of all, nobody got me mixed up in anything, I chose to be here," responded Rob. "Secondly, while I may not agree with Daryl leaving you guys hanging, Phoebe's right. It's not a total waste that we're here. Something is still out there hurting people, and it's our job to put a stop to it. So no one is going home until this is resolved."

"Fine, whatever. I'm going to bed. It's been a long day and even longer night." John stormed out of the room, slamming the door shut behind him.

CHAPTER THREE

June 7, 2017

John awoke to a long, loud creak. He lifted his head up slightly and squinted his sleep-laced eyes, trying to see what it was. Phoebe walked into the room, carrying a box of Dunkin' Donuts and a coffee.

"Morning, Sleeping Beauty," she said as she set the box of donuts and coffee down on a small, round table. "Didn't expect you to be awake yet."

"Yeah, well, with the way you open doors how can I not be? What are you doing, by the way? It's like..." John glanced at the old alarm clock on the nightstand, "seven A.M." He was seriously surprised to see Phoebe up and at 'em, especially considering the time they went to bed. His sister wasn't typically a morning person. In fact, he had to be the one to force her out of bed sometimes.

"I couldn't sleep, so I decided to go for some breakfast. Hey, since you're up, what say we go scope out that bridge?"

"Did you even get any sleep?"

"I got some, yes. Now come on, let's go."

"Phoebe, it's super early. I don't even think Uncle Rob is awake yet, shouldn't we wait for him?"

"Nah, we can do this alone. We're just looking

around. Plus, it'd be nice to spend some time together just the two of us, we haven't seen each other in so long."

John sighed. As tired as he was, he knew he wouldn't be getting back to sleep any time soon, so they might as well go.

"Alright. Give me a minute." He threw the covers off his body and got out of bed.

The Oldsmobile came up on a stretch of road with an old, rusty bridge ahead of it, which was occupied by two cop cars and three officers.

"Well, would you look at that," said Phoebe. She pulled the car over, and she and John took a long look at the scene in front of them before she shut off the engine. Phoebe opened the glove box, took out a box, and opened the lid. It was filled with ID cards—FBI, DEA, US Marshals, Department of Homeland Security, you name it—mostly with her or Daryl's faces on them, though there were a few with John's. Phoebe rifled through the mess of cards and picked two out–one for herself and one for John.

"Let's go," she said.

She and John got out of the car and walked confidently onto the bridge and up to the officers, as if they were supposed to be there. However, the three seemed to be a little too busy to notice the two intruders behind them. One of the officers, a man who had a sheriff insignia on the sleeve of his jacket, leaned over the railing, while the other two, a man and woman, huddled around a third vehicle. The inside of it was covered in blood.

"Any sign of the head?" The sheriff yelled down.

"Nada," came a distant voice from below the bridge.

The male officer next to the car clicked his tongue. "Damn, look at this mess. This guy sure did a number on that poor woman."

Phoebe whistled, catching the attention of all three officers. They turned to face her.

"Woo-wee, looky here," she said as she sauntered around the car, inspecting it. "You boys--and gal, sorry didn't mean to be exclusive—got another one?"

The sheriff looked at her and John quizzically. "And who the hell are you?" he asked.

Phoebe flashed her badge.

"Hmm. Never seen FBI agents so young," said the sheriff.

"And since when does the FBI take interest in small town murders?" asked the female officer.

"Since we heard you guys are apparently sucking at your jobs lately," responded Phoebe.

John chuckled nervously. "Forgive my partner, she seems to forget her manners sometimes." He threw his sister a look. "So what can you tell us about this recent one?"

"Not much. Happened late last night, exact same MO. Woman, head cut clean off, no sign of it. Sick bastard must've run off with it like before," said the sheriff.

"I'll tell you what, though, this guy isn't as sharp as he used to be," said the male officer.

"Oh yeah? Why's that?" asked Phoebe.

"He slipped up. There was another woman in the car with our victim, and he let her get away. A passerby said he found her passed out a distance from the bridge pretty banged up and brought her to the hospital."

"Huh. What's the woman's name? What did she have to say?" Phoebe asked.

"Macy Jones. And no clue yet. One of our officers went over to the hospital just this morning to interview her. Hopefully he got something that'll help us finally catch this S.O.B. Say, if you two want, you're welcome to come down to the station and look over any information he got," said the sheriff.

"Thank you, but we've got this. What's the name of this hospital?"

"Jefferson Healthcare."

John nodded at the three officers. "Thanks for all your help, officers," he said.

Phoebe and John walked off. Phoebe drew her phone out of the pocket of her jacket, pulled up Rob's contact, and hit call. It picked up after the first ring.

"Uncle Rob, John and I are down at the bridge, we came to check it out. Found it riddled with cops, there's been another one… late last night, according to the popo. Oh, and get this, there's a witness, a chick named Macy Jones…. All I know is that she was in the car with the victim, managed to escape, and is now at the local hospital. So get ready, we're coming to get you. We need to get down to that hospital, ASAP."

Phoebe hung up the phone and stuffed it back in her pocket.

"Man, this all still makes me so uncomfortable," said John.

"What does?"

"*This.* Impersonating law enforcement officials."

"Nature of the job, Johnny. You better get used to it, this is officially your life now."

John quickly moved in front of Phoebe, forcing her to stop walking.

"That's what you think. I'm not gonna be doing this the rest of my life."

"Oh yeah? Then tell me, big man, what else you plan on doing?"

"Going to college. I got accepted into Harvard, full ride. Come this September, that's where I'll be."

John stalked off toward the car. Phoebe watched him for a minute or so, sighed, and followed after him.

John, Phoebe, and Rob, dressed in black suits, walked onto a hospital floor and up to the nurses station.

"Excuse me, hi," said John. He flashed his FBI badge. "We're looking for a Macy Jones, we were told she'd be on this floor. We'd like to speak with her about her attack."

"Right this way," said one of the nurses.

She stepped out from behind the station and led them down to one of the rooms. Inside, a young woman laid on the bed, staring intently out the window, as if deep in thought. The nurse gently tapped on the door, and the woman shifted her gaze in their direction.

"Hi, Macy, some agents are here to see you. They want to ask you some questions about what happened. Are you feeling up to it?"

"Sure, why not," replied Macy.

The nurse moved aside, and the three stepped inside the room.

"Hello Macy, I'm Special Agent Forbes with the FBI, these are my partners, Agent Montgomery and Agent Wells. How are you feeling?" said Phoebe.

"Honestly, I've been better. Listen, I already told that other police officer all that I remember."

"We know, but we'd very much appreciate if you could tell us again. We really want to catch the person responsible for doing this to you and to the countless others."

Macy let out a laugh. "I highly doubt you're gonna be able to do that."

"Why is that?"

Macy shook her head. "You wouldn't believe me, it's too crazy."

Phoebe came forward. "Macy, trust me, there's nothing you could say that would sound too crazy. We've heard it all. So go ahead, try me".

Macy keenly gazed at Phoebe. "Alright," she

sighed. "I didn't even tell the other cop this because I knew he wouldn't believe me, but late last night my friend Jennifer and I were on the way home after a night out. Jennifer was driving. We got to McArthur Bridge, and something strange started happening to the car, it kept stopping and starting. It did this a couple of times before completely giving out on us. Jennifer was busy trying to crank the engine when I spotted him. The axeman."

"The axeman?" responded Phoebe.

"Yeah, it's some local legend. A guy was apparently killed on the bridge many years ago. They say he's still out there, that he carries an axe and uses it to cut off the heads of his victims. I never believed it to be true until last night. Anyways, he appeared in front of our car, circled it about three times, and then just disappeared. I thought he was gone but then he suddenly popped up in the back seat. He ch-chopped Jennifer's head clean off, and, and, I'm sorry, oh God, Jennifer!"

Macy put her face in her hands and sobbed. Phoebe put a comforting hand on her shoulder.

"It's okay, Macy, you don't have to say any more. We've heard enough. We'll be out of your hair and let you rest."

The three exited the room. They curtly nodded on their way past the nurses' station and got onto one of the elevators.

Phoebe, back in her regular clothes, sat on one of

the old armchairs in her and John's motel room, her feet kicked up on a small coffee table and a laptop in her lap opened to *The Port Townsend Daily* archive search page. John and Rob, likewise in their regular clothes, sat at the table, grouped around John's laptop, also on the same webpage. Phoebe began to type "man murdered" into the archive's search bar when John uttered "here's something."

"Well, that was quick," Phoebe muttered, she put her laptop aside and went to join John and Rob at the table, standing behind the two. "What you got?"

"An article titled *Local Man Murdered on McArthur Bridge*, dated December 9, 1990," said Tom.

"What's it say?"

John moved the laptop in between him and Rob so that all three of them could read the article.

> *A local man, Edward "Ed" Warner, 40, was found dead on McArthur Bridge earlier this week. His death has been ruled a murder by the sheriff's office. His killer, Jake Hendricks, 21, willingly turned himself in soon after committing the act. In his statement to police, Hendricks alleges that Warner was a serial killer who targeted women in particular and Hendricks was his accomplice who was mainly responsible for picking out the women. Hendricks stated that "after I found out that he had his sights set on my girlfriend, I knew I had to put a stop to him. So I had him meet me at McArthur bridge under the guise that I had found him another potential victim. I then shot him dead." Hendricks has agreed to work with the local*

police and help them uncover where the victims were disposed of in an attempt to lessen his sentence. The Port Townsend Daily has reached out to Mr. Warner's brother, Richard Warner, for a comment but have got no response.

"Huh. If he was a serial killer in his past life who only preyed on women, that would explain why all of his victims on the bridge were women," uttered Rob.

"So, stakeout at the bridge tonight, anyone?" said Phoebe, pointing her index finger back and forth between John and Rob.

They were parked a couple yards down from the bridge. In the darkness of the car, the three sat in silence, watching the bridge. John sighed and turned to Phoebe.

"So what do we do if our friendly neighborhood axeman shows his face?" he asked.

"What do you mean?" replied Phoebe. "We don't do anything. We sit back, we watch, and we learn. First we figure out what we're dealing with, then we figure out how to kill it. Come on, John, you know how this works." Phoebe reached over and popped open the glove compartment. "Can you shine your light for me real quick? There's a bag of chips I put in the glove compartment earlier I wanna grab."

John pulled out his iPhone and turned on the flashlight.

"You guys want one? I brought enough for everybody."

"I'm good," said John.

"Uncle Rob?...." Getting no response, Phoebe turned to look behind her. "Uncle Ro--" she burst out laughing.

"What?" asked John.

"He's knocked out back there."

John craned his neck to see Rob with his head against the window and his mouth slightly opened. He chuckled.

Phoebe snapped her fingers in Rob's face. "Yo!" she cried.

Rob jolted awake. "What? What? What's happening?"

"Have a nice nap there, grandpa?" she teased.

Rob palmed his eyes. "Come on, man, give me a break. I'm old, it's been years since I've done something like this. What do you want? Did our friend show up?"

"Nope. Just wanted to see if you wanted some chips."

"No, I'm okay. I am gonna go take a leak though."

Rob stepped out of the car and made his way around it into the woods. As Phoebe reached into the glove compartment, John caught sight of the bow-and-arrow tattoo on her forearm. A feeling of uneasiness instantly hit him. That tattoo reminded him of his uncle's expectations, and that he would soon have to find some way to explain that he would be breaking free of those expectations and pursuing his own path. And he knew how well that was going to go. But he didn't have much time to dwell on it because on the bridge, a man with a long axe had made an appearance. He stood by the railing, peering over the edge.

"Phoebe."

"What?"

"Look."

Phoebe lifted her head, and John pointed her in the direction of the bridge.

"Oh, shoot."

The axeman climbed over the top of the railing and jumped off.

"Let's go!" Phoebe leaped out of the car and took off towards the bridge. John flung open the door and scrambled out of the car.

"Wait! Wait! What happened to hanging back and— damn it." He rushed after his sister, who was already way ahead of him. John had barely set foot on the bridge when he froze at the sight of Phoebe climbing up on the rail.

"Phoebe– what the hell are you doing?"

She didn't answer him. She stood still for a second, took a long, deep breath, and jumped. A splash echoed up from below.

"Oh my God." John raced to the rail. Phoebe crawled out of the water and collapsed onto her back in the mud, sputtering and muttering something he couldn't make out.

"Phoebe!"

"What?"

"You alright?"

Phoebe held up a hand in an A-OK sign. "Just peachy."

John laughed, relieved. "You're insane, dude, why the hell did you jump?"

"Because he went that way." Phoebe pointed behind her to where the axeman had run off.

"There's a small path right at the end of the bridge."

"Okay, Mr. Know-it-all. Come on, before we lose him." Phoebe pulled herself up and took off in the direction the axeman had gone. John followed suit down the path, whizzing past trees and shrubs until he caught up with Phoebe. The two slowed, panting, trying to catch their breaths. "Where'd you go?" Phoebe muttered, eyes scanning the area. They heard the rustle of footsteps behind them and swiftly spun around.

"Relax, it's just me." Rob made his way over to them. He had the flashlight on his phone on. "How the hell you guys make it all the way here with no light? How are you seeing anything?"

"Where'd you come from?" Phoebe asked him.

"I saw someone go down that clearing by the bridge. Car was empty, figured it was you two, so I followed. Why you all filthy?"

"She jumped from the bridge," said John.

"Why'd you do that?"

"Casper the friendly ghost decided to make his debut. We're tailing him. We've lost him now."

"I see. Why didn't you just take the small path?"

"That's what I said!" said John.

"Oh enough about that path!" cried Phoebe,

annoyed that they kept bringing it up. "I'm an idiot, I know. I should've noticed it. Jeez Louise. You guys are so--"

"There!" shouted Rob, pointing his light behind them to where the axeman had materialized, his back to them. Phoebe and John whirled around. The axeman darted deeper into the woods. The trio sprang after him, dodging low-hanging branches and fallen logs, their path slightly illuminated by the light on Rob's phone. They were gaining on him when he suddenly broke left.

"That way!" cried Phoebe. They took a sharp turn left and stopped. In the distance was an old run-down cabin, but the axeman was nowhere to be seen. "Darn! We lost him. Again."

"Yeah, now we're lost," said John. "How the heck do we get out of here?"

"Maybe this wasn't such a hot idea," said Phoebe.

John threw her a look. "You think?"

CHAPTER FOUR

June 8, 2017

John sat in one of the booths in a busy, local diner, the browser on his laptop opened to the student portal on Harvard's website. Phoebe walked up behind him and briefly glanced at the screen on his laptop before sliding in across from him.

"Watcha doing there?" she asked.

"Some last-minute things for Harvard," said John, his eyes fixated on the computer screen.

Phoebe took a long look at her brother. She had not thought he was being serious when he told her on the bridge that he was going to college. She'd thought he was just blowing smoke, being pissy like he always was when it came to their lifestyle. She had never imagined he would ever actually walk away.

The waitress came over with their food. John quickly put his laptop away.

"Alright, here's a burger for you," the waitress placed the burger down in front of Phoebe. "And a chicken and dumplings for you," and she set the bowl of chicken and dumplings down in front of John.

"Thank you," they both said simultaneously.

The waitress smiled. "You guys enjoy."

"So you're really doing this huh? Freakin' pep

rallies and football games. The whole college boy gig." Phoebe bit down on her burger.

"Well, I don't know about the pep rallies and football games, but yeah, I am."

"I'm assuming you haven't told uncle Daryl yet." She popped some fries in her mouth.

"No."

"Well, you need to. Your eighteenth birthday is in a couple of months. Uncle Daryl's expecting to take you to Eden to get the mark and make your joining the family trade official. Gonna have to tell him you don't plan on sticking around." She took another bite of her burger.

John sighed. "I know, I just... have to think of a good way to tell him. I mean, you know Uncle Daryl, how he'll react. He won't exactly be thrilled."

Phoebe sipped on her soda. "You got that right."

"But honestly, I don't care. This is my life, not his. I'm joining you and him for one final ride this summer–but once September rolls around, I'm done hunting. For good."

Phoebe nodded. She couldn't believe what she was hearing. *Sure, their way of life isn't easy but it isn't that bad. They do a lot of good, help save a lot of people.* And the fact that John was just so willing to turn his back on it all quite frankly irritated the hell out of her.

"So that's it then? You're just gonna bury your past and run off, live some normal apple pie life?"

"Why not? Uncle Rob managed to do it."

Phoebe scoffed. "Yeah, 'cause he's the poster boy

for normalcy. Him and Aunt Laura have been married for what, thirteen years? And she still doesn't know the truth about him, about the things he's done."

"And it's better she never does."

"Lying to your significant other. That's healthy. Word to the wise, Johnny, you can pretend all you want, sooner or later you're gonna have to own up to who you really are."

"Oh yeah? And who am I, exactly?"

"You're one of us. A hunter. One of the so called keepers of the unknown You might not like it, but this stuff is in your blood. You'll never be able to escape it. Not truly."

"Thank you, Master Yoda."

"Oh, eat me."

Phoebe's phone rang, she pulled it out to see who was calling. It was Rob. She answered it.

"Hey Uncle Rob.... You were able to track down the brother, fantastic.... Alright, John and I just got our food, we'll just finish up here and head your way, and we can pay the other Mr. Warner a visit.... Oh you gonna want anything?.... I'll get it."

John, Phoebe, and Rob trekked up the driveway to the front door of a two-story house in a cul-de-sac. Phoebe knocked. An old man in his early seventies answered.

"Yes?" he said.

"Are you Richard Warner?" asked Phoebe.

"Yes."

"Hi, Mr. Warner, I'm Amanda Beck. I'm here with my classmate, Kyle Warren, and our professor, Earl Daniels. We're from the psychology department at Peninsula College. Would we be able to come in?"

"I guess." Richard stepped aside to let them through.

"Thanks, we appreciate it," said John.

He closed the door behind him and led them into the living room.

"May I ask what a couple of psychology students and their professor want with me?"

"We know this might be a sensitive subject for you, Mr. Warner, but my students and I are conducting a study into the minds of serial killers."

"Ah, I see. And you wish to talk to me about Edward."

"Yes sir, as much as you'd be willing to tell us."

Richard took a seat on one of the armchairs. "Please, sit." He gestured between the other armchair and the couch. Phoebe, John, and Rob settled themselves on the sofa. "What would you like to know?"

John cleared his throat. "Well, Mr. Warner, our research seeks to show that serial killers are made, not born. That the environment around them causes them to become what they are. What was Edward's childhood like? Did he experience any kind of traumatic event that could have led to him murdering all of those women?" In all honesty, no one gave a rat's ass about the dude's childhood or his experiences, but they had to come up with some meaningless question to open with, they couldn't jump straight to the point otherwise they'd risk blowing their cover.

"Happy. About as happy, safe, and normal as any child's could be. As for the trauma, if he did I sure as hell never heard anything about it. I just don't know what possessed him to go and do the things he did. We came from a good family, Mom and Dad brought us up with plenty of love."

"Mr. Warner," spoke Phoebe, "where was Edward buried?"

Richard's countenance became confused. "I'm sorry, what does that have to do with your study?"

"Oh our study is gonna come with a paper. We wanna put as much detail of the lives of the people we're researching in there as possible, even down to the nitty-gritty like their burial place," replied Phoebe.

"He wasn't. We had him cremated. Scattered his ashes at some campground our family used to like to go to."

Well that's just great Phoebe thought.

"Was there anything he was attached to? An object, place, person? Something super important to him?" She asked.

"Not that I can think of. It's been years, and my memory has kind of evaded me. If you don't mind, I'm actually kind of tired."

"Of course," said John. "Thanks so much for your time."

As they stood, an old picture on a small round end table next to the couch captured Phoebe's attention.

In it were two young boys and an old man. One of the boys had sandy blond hair and appeared to be about eleven years old, and the other had brown hair and appeared to be about six years old. The old man had an axe slung over his shoulder, his free hand rested on the shoulder of the six-year-old boy. The three wore wide smiles on their faces. But the background was what specifically drew Phoebe to the photograph. In the background was a cabin, the same cabin they encountered in the woods late last night, except it was way more kempt. Phoebe grabbed the picture frame and nudged her elbow into Rob's side. He directed his gaze towards her.

"This cabin look familiar to you?" Phoebe whispered to him. "Um, excuse me, Mr. Warner?" She stepped up to Richard. "I hope you'll forgive me, but I couldn't help but notice this beautiful picture you have here. Is this you when you were a boy?" She handed the frame to Richard. He looked down at it, a small smile formed on his face.

"Yes, this was Ed and I with Grandpa Ted at his cabin near McArthur bridge. I was the sandy-haired one. Plenty of great memories there. Grandpa left it to Ed and I after he died, but Ed was the one who mostly used and took care of it. I ain't been over there since Ed died, though, so it's most likely a mess."

"Your grandpa some kind of lumberjack or something?" Asked Phoebe.

"Oh yeah, grandpa used to love to fell trees and chop wood, he passed that love on to Ed. Ed loved that old thing, grandpa gifted it to him when he was twelve. You asked if there was anything he was attached to, that would be, that would be it, and also the cabin, too."

"Where would the axe be now? Do you have it?" asked John.

"I don't. If I had to guess, down at the cabin. It's where Ed left it after grandpa died. He never used it much since then."

Phoebe nodded. "We appreciate your speaking with us, Mr. Warner. We'll get out of your hair now."

The three exited out the house and strolled down the driveway to the Oldsmobile.

"Well, no body to burn, but we do know ghosts can attach themselves to objects," said Phoebe. "Seems that axe was real special to him. I bet it's what he's attached to."

"We've gotta get down to that cabin, pronto," said Rob.

"Crap," groaned Phoebe. "How the hell are we gonna get back there? We don't even know its exact location, just that it's around the bridge."

"Don't worry, I got this," said John. He drew out his phone and opened up Google Earth. He typed McArthur Bridge, Port Townsend, WA into the search engine. It took him to an aerial image of the bridge. He scrolled past what seemed to be endless trees before landing on a blurry image of the Warner cabin and the road that led up to it. "Found it. Address for Grandpa Ted's cabin is 1307 Shelton Drive."

"Well, what are we waiting for?" said Phoebe, walking over to the driver's side door and opening it. "Put that baby into a GPS and let's move." She got into the car.

"Okay," said John, glancing down at the GPS on his phone. "Turn right up here." He motioned to a road that would be pretty easy to miss if one weren't paying attention.

Phoebe turned onto the road John had pointed out. It was a gravel road and made for a long drive up to the cabin. She put the car in park and shut down the engine. They got out and walked to the trunk. Phoebe lifted the lid, they each grabbed a headlamp as well as a shotgun and filled the barrels with rock salt. John reached for a mini-flamethrower. Rob grabbed an iron crowbar. Phoebe shut the trunk. They strode up to the front door of the cabin. Phoebe turned the door knob and found that it was stuck. She turned harder, slamming her shoulder into the door, putting her back into it. It flew open with a loud bang as it hit the back wall.

"Hey! What the hell, man!" Came a loud cry from inside the cabin along with what sounded like a group of people trying to hurry to their feet. Phoebe, John, and Rob entered, turning on their headlamps. A bunch of startled teenagers stood frozen, bongs and weed littered the floor around them.

"Cops!" one of them screamed.

"Alright boys and girls, fun's over," said Rob. "We

won't arrest you, if you high-tail it out of here. Now." The teenagers scurried out the door. Rob sighed. "Teenagers, I swear. Right, we gotta think, where would this guy keep this axe?"

"Well, it had sentimental value to him," said John, "so he wouldn't store it just anywhere. It would most likely be hanging up on a wall or carefully put away in a closet or any kind of storage chest."

"Okay, let's split up and each search a different area of the cabin, that way we'll cover more ground. Thoroughly check the closets and any room you can find. John and I'll take the right side, Phoebe you take the left."

They set off to their respective sections. John and Rob searched the first bedroom, nothing. They moved onto the second bedroom, still nothing. Meanwhile, Phoebe had just finished in the kitchen, where she'd searched every square inch and got bupkis. She went out into the living room and scoured the area. To her left side, she noticed a door across from her. She moved to it and opened what she assumed would be a coat closet. To her surprise, it led to a basement. She proceeded down.

"Ugh, God," Phoebe gagged. "What in the world?" The entire room reeked of mold, something putrid–and death. She spotted a wooden storage chest on the other side of the basement. She made her way over to it. She undid the latches on the chest and raised the top. Inside were the heads of all of Ed's bridge victims.

"Oh, shit," Phoebe uttered. She covered her nose with the back of her hand. "Well, now we know what he did with the heads. And where the stench is coming from." She quickly shut the chest and pushed on with her search. She thought she hit another dead end, until she saw it, an axe mounted on the wall in front of her.

"There you are." Just as Phoebe reached for it, she felt a cold presence right next to her. She turned. There stood the axeman, grinning.

"You're very beautiful," said the axeman. "Your head will go nicely in my collection."

"Buddy, you have got to work on your flirting skills. It's ass. And I'd hate to be the bearer of bad news, but if anyone's losing their head today, it's you."

Phoebe fired her shotgun at him. He flickered and vanished. Phoebe slung her gun over her back, snatched the axe, and booked it for the stairs only to be intercepted by the axeman. He forcibly seized the handle and yanked it towards him. Phoebe's grip slightly wavered and she staggered forward. She tightened her hold on the axe and jerked it back in her direction. The axeman took one hand off the axe and shoved Phoebe in the chest, hard, flinging her on her back and knocking the wind out of her. As she tried to catch her breath he appeared above her, axe raised, poised to strike.

Rushed, heavy footsteps pounded down the stairs. She heard John call her name. She lifted her head and saw her brother and Rob standing halfway down. The axeman turned to face them, growling. Rob shot at him. He dispersed. John slung his shotgun over his shoulder and ran over to his sister.

"Hey, you okay?" He gave her a hand up.

"Yeah, I'm okay. Just got all the air knocked out of me is all. Man, I had the axe—he took it."

"That's alright," said Rob. "He'll show his ugly face again, we'll get him then."

Almost instantaneously, the axeman reemerged in their midst. He swung the axe at them, they ducked. John dropped the flamethrower and lunged for the axe. He managed to grab the end of the handle, but the axeman roughly pulled back and jabbed the end of the axe into the bridge of his nose. John stumbled back, blood gushing down his face.

"Ahh," he hissed, gingerly touching the wounded area. "Look out!"

The axeman brought the axe down on Phoebe. She dodged and sprang for the weapon, laying hold of it. Rob hurried to join her. Together, they wrestled over the axe with the axeman. John unslung the shotgun from around his shoulder and fired at the axeman, who disappeared, leaving the axe in Phoebe and Rob's hands.

"John, torch it!" cried Rob. He and Phoebe tossed the weapon at John's feet. The axeman, now back beside Phoebe and Rob, snarled and advanced in John's direction. John quickly picked up the flamethrower and set the axe ablaze. The axeman let out a guttural roar as he went out in a burst of flames.

"Booyah! That's how it's done, baby!" Phoebe hollered. "Putting a stop to these evil S.O.B.s never gets old."

John lightheartedly shook his head at his sister, a small grin on his face.

"By the way, you good John?" Phoebe asked him, gesturing to the wound on his face.

"Oh yeah, I'm fine. Just a tiny scratch, nothing I can't handle."

"That's right!"

"Well, let's hurry up and get gone," said Rob, leading the way to a half-lite door. "I don't want to be down here any longer than necessary, it smells awful. What on earth is that?"

"Oh, it's coming from that storage chest over there," said Phoebe, nodding in its direction as they passed by. "It's where old Eddy stashed the heads of all the women he murdered on the bridge."

Rob opened the door. They ascended the bulkhead stairs and stepped out into the back of the cabin. The three circled around to the Oldsmobile. As they reached the car, Rob's phone rang— it was Laura. He answered.

"Hey sweetheart.... Everything's fine around here.... Yes we were able to track down Daryl.... Actually, we're heading home today so I'll fill you in when we get there okay?... Love you too." He hung up. "Let's put as many miles as possible between us and this town, kids. I've had enough excitement here to last me a lifetime."

The three of them climbed into the Oldsmobile and drove off.

Phoebe pulled the car into Rob and Laura's driveway. They made their way inside the house.

"Laur!" Rob called from the entryway.

Laura walked out of the kitchen to greet them, a warm smile on her face. "Hey, you guys! I was so worried about you" She hugged and kissed Rob, then embraced Phoebe and John. "How's Daryl? Is he okay? What happened to him?"

"He's fine, Aunt Laura, no need to worry," said Phoebe. "He just went out to hunt some deer with a couple of his old buddies and lost track of time. Cell signal was pretty shoddy at their cabin, which is why we couldn't reach him before. He had to skedaddle to another job, so he couldn't stop in to say hi, but he sends you his well wishes."

"Well, it's too bad that he couldn't come visit, but I'm happy that he's alright."

"Speaking of, John, we should hit the road. You have anything you need to get?"

"What's the rush, you just got here?" Said Laura.

"Sorry, Aunt Laura but we should really try to meet up with our uncle so we can help him with the job. Our line of work, it's always easier when you have more than one person."

"Actually, Phoebe," said John, "Uncle Daryl made it perfectly clear that he didn't need our help and could handle this job on his own. So I say we hang back and wait for him to call us when it's over, like he said he would. And I'm gonna need more time to gather my things anyway."

Frustration crossed Phoebe's face. She quickly suppressed it—she didn't want Aunt Laura to pick up on it. But why did her brother have to be so stubborn? Especially when it came to their uncle and the family trade? She was trying to do a good thing, go find their uncle so they could help him. And here John was, fighting her every step of the way.

"You heard the man," said Laura, "stay. I made lunch, and there's cheesecake."

Any irritation Phoebe felt at John's bullheadedness diminished as soon as Laura mentioned one of her favorite desserts.

"You had me at cheesecake."

Everyone chuckled and headed for the kitchen.

www.ingramcontent.com/pod-product-compliance
Lightning Source LLC
LaVergne TN
LVHW052343100826
845147LV00021B/1167

* 9 7 8 1 6 2 8 0 6 4 7 2 8 *